We Like the Sun

Written by Ena Keo

STECK-VAUGHN
ELEMENTARY · SECONDARY · ADULT · LIBRARY

A Harcourt Classroom Education Company

www.steck-vaughn.com

Ducks like the sun.

Ducks like the rain.

4

Penguins like the sun.

Penguins like the snow.

Sea gulls like the sun.

Sea gulls like the fog.

8

We like the sun!